THE WINDOWMAKER, THE ... AND
the Sex ...

RETURN TO PLANET METAL

THE SECOND HEAVY METAL FAIRY-TALE
BY
JERRY METAL

ILLUSTRATED BY MIKE BASTIN

First published in Great Britain 17/04/2007
by Rivetthead Publishing, 44 Salisbury Street,
St George, Bristol BS5 8ED.

Printed by Philtone Litho Limited, Bristol

Written by Jeremy D Stephens,
writing under the name Jerry Metal

Typeset in Tiffany Demi.
Additional typesetting in Yokkmokk

ISBN 0-9549861-1-3

www.sexgodsfromplanetmetal.com
jerstephens@hotmail.com

RIVETTHEAD PUBLISHING

For Ma & Pa.
I love you both.

Also by the author:

*The Windowmaker, the Codpiece
and the Sex Gods from Planet Metal
- a Heavy Metal Fairy-Tale*

And so...

...after his recent adventure, Nestor's life returned to normal and he continued to make the finest windows in all the land.

Since his battle with the evil wizard, people came from miles around to marvel at his magical codpiece and hear how he had saved the King's daughter from peril.

Nestor was now so busy that he had to take on an apprentice to help with his many window orders. His apprentice was called Adrian Musculus and together they continued to make the most beautiful windows in all the Kingdom.

But even with all his success, Nestor was sad and carried a heavy heart.

It had been months since his adventure with his friends 'The Sex Gods from Planet Metal', and he longed to see them again. Their tales of bravery and adventure were far more exciting than his life as a humble windowmaker.

But the Knights had been summoned home by their Queen, Queen Aluminium II, and he had not heard from them since.

So Nestor continued to make his beautiful windows and was sad.

One night, after a hard day of windowmaking, Nestor slumbered deeply, his head resting on the voluminous bosom of his beloved wife Muntella.

All was quiet and all was peaceful.

Suddenly, from outside, there came an almighty noise and the room was filled with a blinding light. It was so bright that Nestor thought the sun itself had fallen from the heavens and that the end of the world was upon him.

"Has the Wizard returned to kill me?" cried Nestor hiding under the bed. "Or is it a horde of monstrous vegetables hell bent on revenge?"

Quickly overcoming his fear, Nestor approached the window to see what could be causing such a commotion, and an amazing sight did meet his eyes ...

Floating above his garden was a flying machine of wondrous invention.

It had the likeness of a sailing ship with wings that flapped and wheels that spun, and clouds of steam belched from a chimney at its rear, filling the air with acrid fumes.

Nestor was very scared for he was only wearing his pants but he hurried downstairs as fast as he could whilst Muntella stayed inside and hid in the wardrobe.

Opening the front door, he arrived in the garden just as the flying machine came to rest on his beloved compost heap. So picking up a broomstick he bellowed in his bravest voice, "Be gone from my garden you flying fiend and damage my compost heap no more!"

But he received no reply and after a moment grew angry, waving his broom in the air and shouting, "State thy business or face the wrath of Nestor, windowmaker to the King!"

And Nestor did ready himself for battle.

Suddenly, a drawbridge creaked open in the side of the craft and a multi-headed silhouette appeared in the doorway filling Nestor with dread.

"What manner of beast is this?" he cried in desperation.

"Am I to meet my end thus? Will I ever see my beloved Muntella again?" And Nestor prepared for the worst.

Then a voice boomed out from the doorway which stopped him in his tracks. "Friend Nestor! Does thou not recognise your comrades in adventure?"

Nestor dropped his broom in amazement, for he recognised the voice at once.

"Does my beard deceive me? Can it be?" cried Nestor in disbelief.

'THE SEX GODS FROM PLANET METAL have returned!"

And for the moment all was well and he completely forgot about the damage to his compost heap.

His friends descended the ramp and greeted him with a hearty embrace. Then, after they had secured their ship, they headed into the house for an early morning tankard of ale.

And there they sat before him, just as he remembered them:

'THE SEX GODS FROM PLANET METAL':

Sir David of Rivett, with his dashing good looks and tattooed skin.

Anthony Strongbeard with his Quad String Thunder Axe and voluminous stomach.

Squeeker, son of Squeeker, with his earth-shaking Drums of Doom.

And last but not least, Jason Quickfinger with his enchanted lute and handsome stack boots.

His friends were back and Nestor was happy.

Meanwhile...

Nestor's apprentice Adrian Musculus was awoken by the
same terrible noise that had awoken Nestor and he too
wondered what it was.

Adrian lived in a small shed nearby and when he had dressed
he set off quickly to find the cause of the mysterious hullabaloo.

When he arrived, he too saw the wondrous flying machine
and approached the craft in search of his master.

"Master Nestor, are you there? It is your faithful apprentice
Adrian," he whispered. But no reply came, so he called
out again. Still no reply.

"Maybe he is inside?" thought Adrian and with that he crept
into the flying machine in search of his master...

Meanwhile...

Back in the house, the knights drank their ale, while Nestor quickly dressed upstairs. When he returned he couldn't help but ask: "Brave friends, where have you been? It has been so lonely here without adventure." For he had missed them all greatly.

"We have just returned from our beloved homeland," said Sir David of Rivett, sounding most grave.

"All is not well on Planet Metal," said Squeeker, son of Squeeker.

"What is wrong?" asked Nestor, "Does a dragon need slaying? Do some unruly vegetables need punishing? Or perhaps... you need some windows for your castle?" he added hopefully.

"Our plight is greater than mere windows," said Jason Quickfinger.

"And involves skullduggery most treacherous," added Anthony Strongbeard.

So when Nestor had refilled their drinks, Sir David retold their story most grim.

The Queen's advisor, Baron Horatio Von Cripplecock, had hatched an evil plan to overthrow the Queen. He had assembled an army of mechanical soldiers with the help of an evil toy maker, and was laying siege to the Royal Palace.

Luckily one of the Queen's Royal Dwarfs had escaped and sent word to the brave Knights, who stole a Sky Galleon and made haste to the house of Nestor where they all now sat, in moods most foul.

Nestor was saddened at their news and vowed to help. "Brave friends, you only have to ask and I will stand ready at your side, but what can I do against mechanical soldiers? I am only a humble windowmaker after all."

To which the Knights replied:

"We need your arm most strong!" cried Anthony Strongbeard.

"And your bravery supreme!" added Jason Quickfinger.

"But most of all..." said Squeeker, son of Squeeker.

"We need your Codpiece of Power!" added Sir David.

And with that they all applauded.

After such flattery, Nestor agreed immediately, for it was the least he could do for his friends.

He took a small whistle from his tunic and summoned his enchanted codpiece from its resting place on the mantlepiece behind him.

"We cannot waste another moment!" cried Nestor. "Let us away at once and rescue the Queen!"

"WE MUST RETURN TO PLANET METAL!"

But first he would have to tell his wife he was off on another adventure, and Nestor was scared.

So the brave Knights returned to their Sky Galleon and made ready to depart whilst Nestor went upstairs and told his wife he was going away... again.

When she heard the news she wailed and she screamed
and she gnashed her teeth in a rage most foul.

Muntella was very cross indeed, for Nestor had promised to
take her shopping for a new glass eye that very morning.

Nestor explained he was honour-bound to the knights for
they had helped him before, but Muntella didn't care and hit
him on the head with a mechanical bed toy she had nearby.

Nestor left the house quickly and could still hear Muntella's
shrieking as he boarded the knights' flying machine, his head
still hurting from where she had hit him.

Finally, when they were ready to depart, Nestor asked the
Knights, "How do we get to Planet Metal? I have never seen
your wondrous kingdom and cannot find it on any map!"

"Fear not, my friend," said Jason Quickfinger, "My magical lute
will show us the way!"

And with that Jason picked up his instrument and by
strumming a mystical spell, opened a vortex high in the night
sky above them.

"Prepare to cast off!" cried Sir David, and Nestor watched in
awe as Anthony Strongbeard pulled levers and turned dials
until the flying machine arose from the ground and flew into
the swirling vortex overhead.

Just as they were leaving, Nestor looked out of his porthole and saw that the door to Adrian Musculus's shed was open.

"How strange?" thought Nestor, "I wonder what Adrian is doing up so early?"

But before he could think another thought they were all whisked away, and he forgot all about his wife, his windows and his young apprentice.

Nestor did not know where they were.

He looked out of the porthole at the strange sky passing by and was scared. It was filled with wondrous colours that moved with a likeness of the sea, and strange creatures could be seen swimming in the clouds just outside his window.

The knights saw their friend was scared and sought to comfort him.

"Fear not Nestor," cried Sir David, "We are on a cosmic thoroughfare between your world and ours which cannot be found with any chart or compass."

"It is a place frequented by Sky Riders and Thunder Thieves," explained Anthony as he piloted the ship onwards through the vortex.

Nestor did not know what they were talking about, and it all sounded very frightening to a humble windowmaker. So he sat back in his chair and tried to enjoy the ride as best he could whilst the knights continued to pilot their flying machine, pulling levers and turning dials.

A short while later there was a large bump and the knights uttered a lusty cry, for they had emerged from the vortex high above Planet Metal.

"Set us down out of sight
So we can plan, before we fight
Quickly now, before we're seen
Or we'll fail to save the Queen!"

They cried, and with that they landed in a small courtyard on the outskirts of the Royal Palace, far away from prying eyes.

When they had secured the ship and made it hidden they sat down to devise a plan with which to rescue the Queen.

After many minutes, Nestor had an idea.

"Jason's mystical lute can transport us into the Queen's chambers, and once inside, we can rescue her!" he suggested, feeling very clever.

But the Palace was protected by many spells and charms to stop just such a plan.

Then Nestor had another idea.

"I could fly us over the battlements with my enchanted codpiece and once inside, we can rescue her!" he cried, again feeling very clever.

But the Queen's archers had the keenest eyes and the sharpest arrows and could easily mistake them for assassins.

Finally Nestor had a third idea.

"I shall pose as a travelling windowmaker and trick my way into the Palace, and once inside, we can rescue her!"

The knights thought this a very good idea, all except for Squeeker who thought the plan too dangerous. "Such an approach is madness and fraught with danger! It's like ringing the devil's doorbell!" he exclaimed.

But after much discussion they decided it was the best plan they had and besides, no one else could think of a better one.

So before Nestor left, Jason was sent on ahead to break some Royal windows so that their plan would appear real. Then, as Nestor did not have any tools with him, they filled a bag with turnips with which to fool the guards at the gates.

"How will I let you in?" asked Nestor. "For there are many doors in the Palace and I have not been there before."

Quickly, the knights drew him a map and described a door in the Royal kitchens which led down to the river. The kitchens were usually deserted at night so he should have no problem reaching it and letting them in.

Finally, the time came for Nestor to depart.

He bid farewell to the knights and set off toward the Palace armed with his courage, his codpiece and a bag of turnips.

As he approached the Palace he saw the mechanical soldiers for the first time and was filled with dread. They had the likeness of a man with limbs made of metal and eyes that glowed red. Some walked on legs whilst others had wheels and he could hear the whirring of the cogs inside their hard metal bodies. They looked like mannequins with kill appeal and Nestor had never seen such angry machines.

When he got to the gates, he was stopped by two soldiers who questioned him with cold metallic voices.

"WHO GOES THERE?" asked the one with legs.

"FRIEND OR FOE?" added the one with wheels.

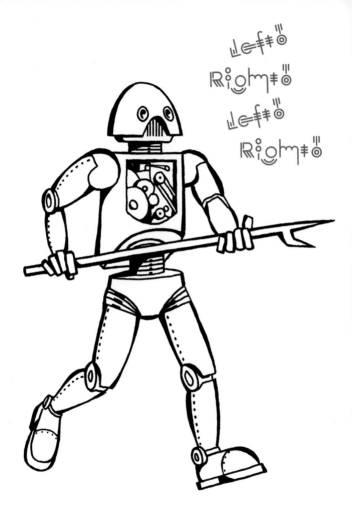

Private Iron, Infantry

Private Chugwell, Mobile division

"I am a travelling windowmaker looking for work," said Nestor hiding his fear and hoping their plan would work. Luckily as Jason had already broken some windows, Nestor was allowed in.

"ⒻⓄⓁⓁⓄⓌ ⓊⓈ." said the one with legs.

"ⓌⒺ ⓌⒾⓁⓁ ⓉⒶⓀⒺ ⓎⓄⓊ ⓉⓄ ⓄⓊⓇ ⓁⒺⒶⒹⒺⓇ."

said the one with wheels, and Nestor was escorted away to meet the Baron.

The Baron was a wicked fellow with the likeness of a twisted tree, and when he saw Nestor he pointed at him with a bony finger and said:

> *Fix my windows like you say*
> *and you'll live to work another day!*
> *The Queen is gone, and now I rule.*
> *Now get to work, you hairy fool!*

Nestor made as if to set to work. Tending to the broken windows as best he could without tools until nightfall when he was given lodgings. Then, at midnight, he crept out of his room, through the Palace kitchens to the door the knights had described.

Then Nestor took out his small whistle and signalled to the knights who had been waiting in a bush near the river.

"Well done Nestor, you are so brave. Let's find the Queen and save the day!" cried Sir David as they set off into the darkness.

The Knights knew the Palace well and took many short cuts. Past the Metal Church, across the courtyard of the Armoured Saint then through the Gardens of Amplification they hurried, almost losing Nestor along the way as he stopped to view these wondrous places.

Shortly, they arrived at the Queen's private chambers but the Queen was nowhere to be found.

The knights searched every room, including her vast cupboards of royal undergarments but still they could not find her.

"This is grave indeed!" said Sir David becoming ever more concerned for his beloved monarch.

Suddenly, they heard a noise behind them and turned, hoping to see their Queen. But instead were confronted by Baron Cripplecock and a number of his mechanical soldiers.

"Ye-Gods!" cried Squeeker at such an awesome sight.

"We've been rumbled!" agreed Anthony Strongbeard, and he was right. They had walked into a trap.

"How did we fail?" exclaimed Nestor, "My plan was foolproof!"

"I have heard of you, windowmaker," said the Baron "And your enchanted codpiece!" Then he let out an evil laugh.

"Did you think you could fool me? For nothing escapes the notice of Baron Cripplecock! Now, prepare to fall at the hands of my soldiers!" and with that, the Baron's mechanised warriors marched forward in a menacing fashion.

As the tidal wave of conflict loomed over them, the Knights stood ready with hearts of courage and faces of grim determination.

"I will crush their cogs," cried Anthony Strongbeard.

"I will smash their springs," cried Jason Quickfinger.

"I will turn them into scrap," cried Squeeker son of Squeeker.

"And give the Baron a hefty slap," added Sir David, and with that both sides did engage, and what followed was both noisy and terrible.

Man against machine, sword against steel, iron will against iron man.

They fought long and they fought hard, but one by one the Knights were overpowered, for the mechanical soldiers were strong and could fight on much longer than mortal men.

"Never have I been so tired," puffed Anthony Strongbeard.

"These metal fiends have strength beyond strength!" added Sir David swinging his sword this way and that as he battled bravely on.

But try as they might they were no match for the Baron's soldiers and as each Knight was captured he was put into a large cage nearby until only Nestor remained free.

Nestor wasn't happy at being left on his own, for he too was becoming tired. So he commanded his codpiece to carry him aloft, lifting him out of reach of the soldiers so he could rest a moment and form a plan.

But the Baron was cunning and summoned archers to knock him out of the sky, for he was evil like that and had anticipated such an event.

Thinking he was doomed, Nestor suddenly remembered the bag of turnips he was carrying and had an idea. Choosing the biggest one he could find, he threw it at the nearest mechanical archer with all his might.

The turnip struck the archer and to his astonishment knocked its head clean off, stopping the metal warrior dead in its tracks.

So Nestor threw another turnip, and another, each time knocking off a soldier's head, for his aim was straight and true.

"Bravo!" cried the Knights from their prison and for a brief moment they tasted the heady nectar of victory.

But the Baron became angry and hatched another evil plot. Shaking his fist skyward he cried:

> *"Return to the ground from whence you came*
> *before I command your friends be slain!"*

And at the Baron's command, the archers turned their arrows on the knights so Nestor could see the danger and see that his plan had failed.

Nestor stopped his turnip assault immediately for he loved his brave friends dearly and did not wish them dead.

Sadly, he returned to the ground and was put into the cage alongside his companions. An echoing clunk resounded as the door was locked and they were all taken off to the deepest darkest dungeon whilst the Baron did a little dance, and was happy for he had won.

The dungeon was very dark and very smelly and their only source of light came from a tiny window high up near the ceiling.

After fruitlessly searching for a means of escape they all became sad and their spirits were low.

Realising they might be here for some time they cursed themselves for not acting sooner against the Baron and his Metal Gods.

"We've taken too much for granted," sighed Anthony Strongbeard.

"And all the time it had grown," agreed Jason Quickfinger.

"We're caught between the hammer and the anvil" wailed Squeeker in dispair, his head in his hands.

"Fear not brave chums," said Sir David, "it's always darkest before dawn. Soon we'll be toasting our victory over these idols of False Metal."

But Nestor thought otherwise and remained quiet whilst outside, the Baron's mechanical soldiers could be heard marching in the streets, dragging iron feet.

After many hours they were suddenly awoken by a noise at the window above.

"Friend Nestor, are you there?" whispered a voice. "It is your faithful apprentice Adrian."

Nestor could not believe his ears and thought he must be dreaming. "I can't believe my ears!" he muttered "I must be dreaming!"

But Nestor was not dreaming. It was indeed his faithful apprentice and he was overjoyed at his timely appearance and demanded an explanation.

Adrian had boarded the Knights' ship looking for Nestor and had fallen asleep. Then when they landed, he awoke and followed at a distance until such time as he could reveal himself.

Invigorated by Adrian's arrival, the Knights hurriedly urged him to free them all.

"How will you get us out? There are mechanical soldiers everywhere." asked Nestor.

"Fear not, Master, this window is not made very well and the bars will only take a moment to remove." And with that, Adrian set to work on the window.

"Thank heavens it is not one of my fine windows," said Nestor "For if it were, it would be too strong to remove and we'd all be stuck here for ever." And the Knights all sighed with relief.

Once Adrian had removed the window he called down again.

"The window is gone but how will I reach you, for I have no rope to lower down?"

None of them had thought of this and once again became disheartened.

But moments later, Sir David made a startling revelation...

"Nestor we are saved!" he cried triumphantly, pointing at Nestor's loins.

"What on earth do you mean?" asked Nestor, clearly mystified.

"Your Codpiece!" exclaimed Sir David, "The Baron has forgotten to confiscate it!"

And the Knights all gasped in amazement for Sir David spoke the truth.

During their battle, the Baron was so happy at capturing the Knights he had forgotten to remove Nestor's codpiece and would now live to regret his mistake.

Quickly, Nestor flew each Knight in turn up to the window so they could all escape.

All went well and quickly, save for Anthony Strongbeard, whose voluminous stomach became stuck in the window and required assistance from the other Knights. But once free, they were all ready and did hunger for battle.

As they made ready to leave, Jason Quickfinger cried out, "Hold fast, metal friends! I hear someone crying nearby."

And the Knights did pause to listen.

"It is coming from the dungeon next to ours!" said Squeeker pointing yonder.

So the Knights investigated and to their amazement found their beloved Queen imprisoned in the dungeon next to theirs.

Through the window they could see her asleep on the floor surrounded by her royal dwarves, one of whom was crying softly in the darkness.

The Knights, relieved to find her alive, called down and threw things until she awoke. And within minutes Adrian was removing the window, before Nestor flew down and lifted them all free.

The Queen was delighted at being rescued as were her dwarves who jumped around in an excitable fashion. But Sir David calmed their high spirits, for they still had to vanquish the Baron before the Queen could return to the throne.

So after much discussion, Adrian escorted the Queen and her dwarves back to their flying machine where they would be safe, whilst the rest of them prepared for battle.

"But how can we fight without our weapons?" asked Jason.

"We have not a mace or cudgel between us!" agreed Squeeker.

"And I am all but naked without my Quad String Thunder Axe!" added Anthony Strongbeard sounding most grim.

But Nestor had a plan and jumped to his feet shouting "To the kitchens...to the kitchens at once!"

"This is no time for feasting!" cried Sir David angrily. "'Tis time for a battle most glorious!"

Nestor quickly calmed Sir David and told him of his plan. He reminded them of his turnip assault against the Baron's soldiers and proposed they used this strategy again.

"In the kitchen I spied a store room full of vegetables," explained Nestor. "And there I saw enough turnips to fell a thousand mechanical soldiers!"

On hearing this the Knights were unsure, for they were unfamiliar with vegetable-based warfare, but after Nestor's recent success they decided to give it a go.

So, moving with stealth, they entered the Palace kitchens and quickly found the storeroom Nestor had spoken of.

Suddenly, from the next room they heard a noise.

"Someone approaches!" whispered Jason and before Nestor could blink the knights had disappeared into thin air, for they were all skilled in the art of concealment.

Unfortunately Nestor wasn't, and he stood around dithering until a cupboard door swung open and from inside Sir David whispered, "Quickly Nestor, get under the table with Squeeker!"

And a moment later they were all concealed.

From under the table Nestor watched as someone entered the kitchen and moved about the room. Suddenly, the lights went out and the sound of a lusty scuffle could be heard under the cover of darkness.

"Seize him!"

"Who's there?"

"Help!"

"Ow!"

"Get off my foot!"

"Get off my beard!"

"Quickly someone, the lights!"

When the lights came on, Nestor saw that Sir David and Anthony had hold of the stranger but released him almost immediately.

From under the table Nestor asked, "Who is this man? And why have you released him?"

To which the stranger replied, "I am Eliot of Osbourne, Chief Piemonger to the Queen of Planet Metal!" And the knights all greeted him like a long lost brother.

Eliot was an old friend of the Knights who had stood firm on many great adventures. His true strength lay in his ability to make the tastiest pies in the whole kingdom and was duely appointed Chief Piemonger and swapped adventuring for cooking.

Eliot was very relieved that the Queen's message had reached them and he relished the chance to fight again. "The Baron is hosting a feast in the Great Hall! Let me lead the way to victory! It will be like old times!" he cried, giddy with excitement.

Sadly, Sir David declined his offer, for being Chief Piemonger, Eliot would surely be missed and his absence could arouse suspicion. Instead, Sir David had a better idea...

He instructed Eliot to smuggle as many turnips as he could into the Great Hall and await their signal when he would be more than welcome to join the battle alongside them.

Then they bid him farewell and made ready to leave.

But before they had reached the door, a metallic cry came from outside.

"TO ARMS! TO ARMS!"

"THE PRISONERS ARE FREE!"

"CALL OUT THE GUARD!"

"HUNT HIGH AND LOW!"

Their escape had been discovered.

"Surely now we are doomed!" wailed Nestor fearing recapture. "Never again will I see my beloved Muntella!"

"'Tis only a matter of time till we are caught!" agreed Jason sensing defeat.

But looking around and thinking swiftly, Sir David cried, "All is not lost! Using these pots and pans we can disguise ourselves as metal soldiers!"

"And victory can still be ours!" added Anthony as he adorned himself in things made for boiling and roasting.

Quickly, Nestor and the Knights created costumes out of all manner of kitchenware, until they resembled the Baron's soldiers and felt very brave indeed.

Then once the coast was clear, they ventured out into the courtyard, walking stiffly and making all manner of metallic noises.

"ᏟᏟᏟᏆᎧᎥᠬᏦ Ꭷ   ᏟᏟᏟᏆᎧᎥᠬᏦ Ꭷ   ᏟᏟᏟᏆᎧᎥᠬᏦ Ꭷ"

"ᏟᏟᏟᠬᎧᎥᎦᠬ Ꭷ   ᏴᎧᎥᠬ Ꮆ Ꭷ   ᏔᏔᏆᠬᎥᏃᏃ Ꭷ   ᏆᎧᏆᎧ Ꭷ"

Fortunately, a group of soldiers were just marching by, and as they passed they fell into line behind them. Now all they had to do was find the Baron.

From beneath the colander on his head Nestor spied many soldiers searching for them. "I hope our disguises work," he thought, as he marched along, yearning to be back in the safety of his workshop making his beautiful windows.

They followed the mechanical soldiers for some time until they entered a huge dining hall filled with many people. And there they saw the Baron, seated with his henchmen, all of whom were enjoying a great feast to celebrate his becoming King.

Many so-called guests were there too, forced against their will to enjoy the celebrations whilst the Baron's mechanical soldiers stood guard, making sure no-one misbehaved.

As fortune would have it, the soldiers they were following marched straight down the hall and stopped right next to the Baron's table. And there the Knights stood, waiting for the right moment to strike...

As the feast progressed, the Knights became restless for there were many courses and toasts to endure. Their disguises were quite uncomfortable and caused chafing in all manner of unmentionable places. Secretly, Nestor wondered how much longer they could hold out.

And he didn't have to wait long to get an answer.

Anthony Strongbeard's costume was a dangerously tight fit and after a while he could not hold his stomach in any more. Suddenly, and with an almighty sound, his costume sprang apart, revealing the portly Knight beneath.

"What is wrong with that soldier?" asked an evil henchman, "he seems to be coming apart!"

"And the one next to him has a cooking pot on his head!" exclaimed another.

"Those are not my soldiers!" shrieked the Baron in amazement. "They are imposters!"

"That's right! We are not your soldiers!" cried Sir David.

"We are THE SEX GODS FROM PLANET METAL!" shouted Squeeker.

"And we've come to reclaim the throne!" added Eliot the Piemonger, emerging from the shadows, dragging a trolley full of turnips behind him.

And with that, they cast off their disguises and prepared for affray.

The Baron was furious at this intrusion and shrieked loudly.

> *"You've escaped me once, but not again,*
> *Prepare to die in lots of pain!"*

Then, he ordered his soldiers to kill them all so they would bother him no more.

But this time the Knights were prepared, and as the soldiers advanced they fought back with bravery and vegetables.

Turnip after turnip was hurled by the Knights and one by one the mechanical soldiers fell, their heads knocked off by the keen eye and strong arm of Nestor and the Sex Gods from Planet Metal.

On they bravely fought until they ran low on ammunition and required replenishment.

"Quickly, to the kitchens for more turnips," cried Sir David heading for the door. So off they ran, followed by the remaining soldiers who marched ever onwards after them.

Upon reaching the kitchens there was barely time to catch their breath, for the Baron's soldiers were right behind them and the Knights did fear for their lives.

Just as defeat seemed inevitable, Nestor had another idea and shouted "Follow me, brave friends, I have a plan that cannot fail!"

And without hesitation, the Knights followed Nestor through the kitchens, out of the door and down to the river's edge.

Fearlessly they waded into the icy water and swam like fish, 'til they reached the other side where they stopped to catch their breath and Nestor prayed that his plan would work.

And it did.

Relentlessly, the mechanical soldiers marched onwards after the Knights. Out of the Palace, down to the river and into the water they went. But mechanical solders aren't built for swimming, and the river was deep and the current was strong.

As the soldiers reached the middle, their footing became uncertain and one by one they were swept away into the murky depths, where their heavy metal bodies sank to the bottom, never to be seen again.

The Baron saw this and tried to stop them, for without his soldiers he could not rule the Kingdom.

"Stop! Stop!" he cried as he ran to the front, trying to push them back with all his might. But the soldiers were too strong and carried on marching, dragging the Baron with them into the river where he quickly drowned and was killed by death.

Then all was silent and Nestor and the Knights knew that they had won.

The Queen and Planet Metal and were saved.

When the Queen received word that the Baron was dead she was very happy and in no time at all she was back on her throne surrounded by her Royal Dwarves. Soon after, the Baron's henchmen were rounded up and order was restored to the Kingdom much to everyone's relief.

So great was her joy, she even forgave the Knights for rifling through her royal undergarments, for it was all done in defence of the realm and was never mentioned again.

And to show her gratitude she threw a huge banquet and ordered her Chief Pie Monger, Eliot, to make the finest pies he had ever made with which to honour her brave rescuers.

Finally, and after much feasting, it was time for Nestor and his apprentice to leave Planet Metal and return to their own world.

There were a great many window orders to be finished and Nestor still had to take his wife shopping for a new glass eye.

So, with help of Jason's magical lute and Anthony's stout piloting, Nestor and Adrian were returned home safe and sound, where Adrian went back to bed and Nestor took his beloved wife shopping.

And when Muntella finally got her new glass eye, she stopped hitting Nestor on the head.

And Nestor was happy.

The End

The End

Acknowledgements

Mike Bolton, Lucy Williams,
Chris 'Bearman' Devanial, Paul Beck,
Chris Bailey, Ian of Primitive,
Roger Hastings, Ian 'Weston' Reason,
Dave Rive#, Anthony 'Moogman' Peacock,
Jason Morris, Ian 'Squeeker' Smith,
Paul Seymours, Robin Askew, Vivienne Weller,
Sally Davies, Kerry Harrison,
Mike Hemmberger
and Julian Priest.

www.sexgodsfromplanetmetal.com
www.sexgodsfromplanetmetal.com